The MYSTERY of the LOST ANCHOR

Written by Michael Murray · Illustrated by Ivan Murphy
Based on a concept by Graham McBride
Edited by Geraldine Hennigar

Nimbus Publishing & The Nova Scotia Museum, Halifax, Nova Scotia, 1993

© Crown copyright Province of Nova Scotia, 1993

93 94 95 96 97 98 6 5 4 3 2 1

Produced as part of the Nova Scotia Museum Program
of the Department of Education, Province of Nova Scotia

Minister: Honourable John D. MacEachern
Deputy Minister: Robert P. Moody

A product of the Nova Scotia Government
Co-publishing Program

Designed by Ivan Murphy
Printed by McCurdy Printing and Typesetting Limited
Produced by the Department of Supply and Services
and the Nova Scotia Museum

Canadian Cataloguing in Publication Data

Murray, Michael, 1955–

The mystery of the lost anchor

Co-published by Nova Scotia Museum
ISBN 1-55109-064-3

I. Murphy, Ivan. II. McBride, Graham, 1931–
III. Nova Scotia Museum. IV. Title.

PS8576.U72M97 1993   jC813'.54

C93-098698-9   PZ7.M87My 1993

ACKNOWLEDGEMENTS

THIS BOOK has been a collective project, developed and nurtured through the contributions of many people.

Graham McBride developed the germ of the story as a label for anchors on display outside the Maritime Museum of the Atlantic. Michael Murray saw its potential as a children's story, wrote the first draft, recruited Ivan Murphy as illustrator, and made his idea a book through unswerving commitment to his vision.

Children's writer Geraldine Hennigar breathed the life and voices of real children into the story. Etta Moffatt and John Hennigar-Shuh contributed a cunning mixture of laughter, good ideas, and moral support. Susan Lucy created the glossary and gave the manuscript a final, helpful, critical read.

Ivan Murphy peopled the story and gave us eyes to see Caitlin, Sean, Robin, Nicole, Captain Bowe, and some very mischievous creatures. His vision, skill, and humour are illustrated on every page.

The Maritime Museum of the Atlantic would like to thank the Captain and crew of the Russian trawler *Vyshgorod* for donating the "Lost Anchor" to the Museum.

"Come on, guys," coaxed Caitlin. "We're almost there!"

"Why are we going to the Maritime Museum? asked Sean. "It's Saturday! I want to have some fun."

"Yeah!" cried Robin. "The place is probably full of boring old stuff."

"Museums are awesome," said Caitlin. "There's lots to see and do."

"Like what?" asked Sean.

"These anchors for starters," she said.

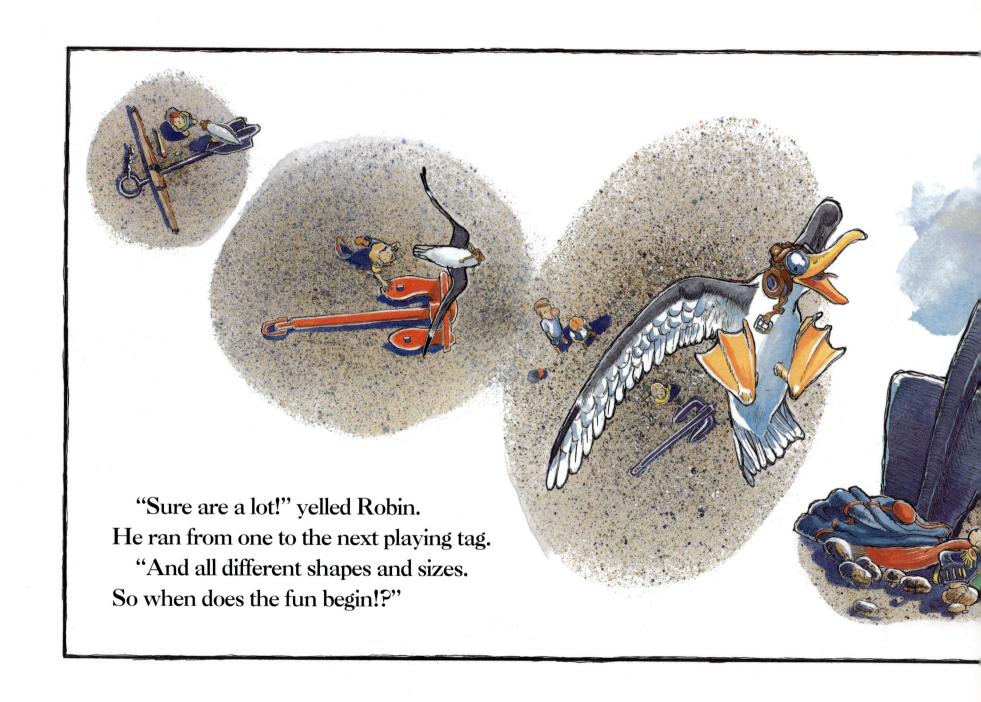

"Sure are a lot!" yelled Robin.
He ran from one to the next playing tag.
   "And all different shapes and sizes.
So when does the fun begin!?"

At that very moment a tall woman, wearing a white lab coat, swung open the doors of the museum. She marched over to a small black anchor with a diamond-shaped hole. Clutched tightly in one hand was a notebook just like Caitlin's. Spectacles slid down her nose each time she stooped to examine the anchor through a magnifying glass.

She looked...

and she looked...

"Aha!" she exclaimed, quickly scratching notes in her book.

"Ohhh," she mumbled aloud, "how can I solve this mystery?"

"Did you say mystery?" asked Robin, running over to the woman.

"I love mysteries," blurted Sean. "Can I help?"

"Sorry if my brothers are bothering you.
I'm Caitlin and I'm looking for something to research."

"We're looking for fun," said Sean and Robin.

"Great," said the woman. "Perhaps we can team up for
some fun research. I'm Nicole Mosher and I have oodles of
questions to ask this little anchor."

"That's silly! Anchors can't talk," laughed Robin.

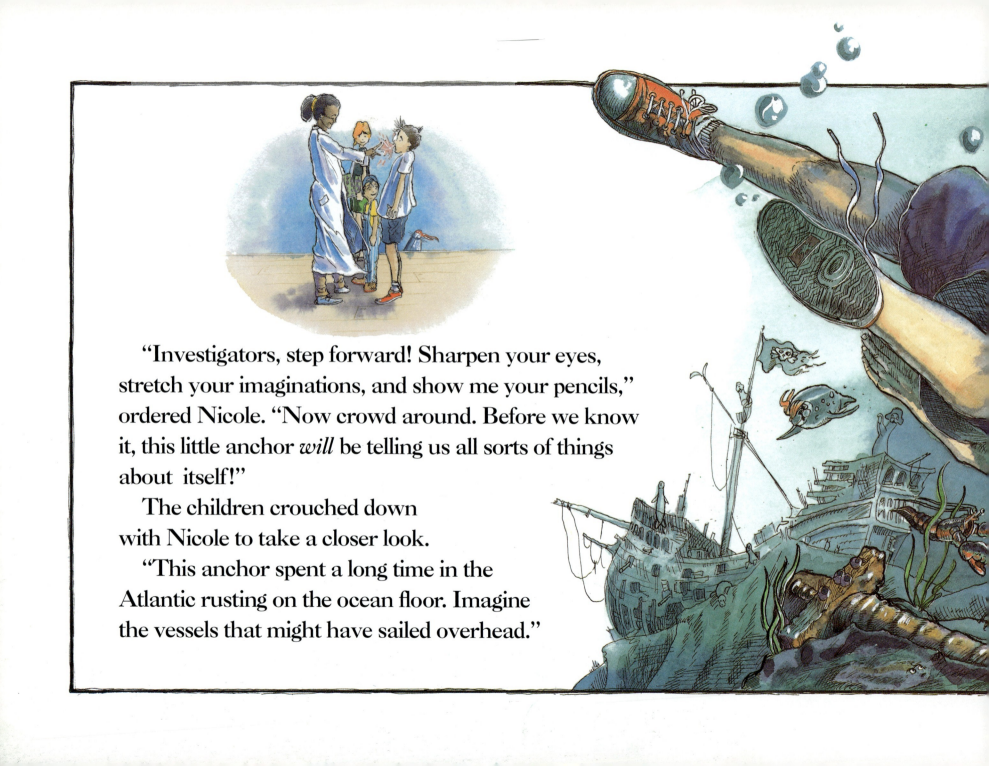

"Investigators, step forward! Sharpen your eyes, stretch your imaginations, and show me your pencils," ordered Nicole. "Now crowd around. Before we know it, this little anchor *will* be telling us all sorts of things about itself!"

The children crouched down with Nicole to take a closer look.

"This anchor spent a long time in the Atlantic rusting on the ocean floor. Imagine the vessels that might have sailed overhead."

Suddenly Nicole snatched a bottle of bubbles
out from Robin's pocket. Taking a deep breath she blew
a bubble for herself and each of the children.

"I can see schooners surrounded by tiny dories fishing for cod,"
said Nicole. "Look, Caitlin, can you see square-rigged ships
bringing hundreds of immigrants to Canada?"

"Why so many?" asked Caitlin.

"Europe was full to bursting with people looking for HOPE,"
answered Nicole. "Homes, Opportunity, Peace, and Employment.
They hoped to find these in Canada.

"Robin, can you imagine early paddlesteamers splashing their
way across the ocean, carrying products and mail from Europe?"

"I've read stories about wartime ships," said Sean.
"Convoys of cargo ships, tankers, and troopships, zigzagging
across the ocean trying to hide from enemy submarines."

"How did the museum get this anchor?" asked Caitlin.
"According to my records," answered Nicole, "it was brought
up in 1989 in the nets of a Russian trawler called the *Vyshgorod*.
They found it just off Sable Island. Goodness knows how
long it lay on the bottom."

"But, where did it come from?" asked Robin.
Nicole scratched above her ear with a pencil.
"I would guess it probably came from a fishing
schooner. Perhaps one like the *Bluenose*."
"The *Bluenose*! That's the ship on the back of the dime!"
announced Robin holding a dime for everyone to see.

"I've heard about Sable Island," said Sean. "They call it
the 'Graveyard of the Atlantic'. Hundreds of ships have been
caught by the winds and currents and smashed on its shores."

"Yes," agreed Nicole sadly. "Our anchor would have been surrounded
by the remains of many an ill-fated ship."

"Okay, brainy brother," said Robin tugging on Sean's sleeve,
"how did the anchor end up on the bottom of the ocean?"

"I don't know," answered Sean honestly.

"And that's one of the mysteries I'm trying to solve," said Nicole.

"Maybe I can be of some help," came a voice from behind them.
"That little fellow is a fisherman's anchor. Museum folk call it an
Admiralty pattern anchor."

"Kids, I would like to introduce you to Captain Joseph Bowe,"
said Nicole. "He works around here."

Captain Bowe set down his duffle bag.
He tipped his cap and shook Caitlin's hand.
"My grandfather was a schooner master
who fished around Sable Island."

Next, he shook Sean's hand.
"He told me lots of stories about
a fisherman's life at sea."

Finally he bent down and looked at Robin, eyeball to eyeball. "I could tell you a story or two about vessels that would have used an anchor just like that one. Do you have the nerve to listen?" "Yes," replied Robin. "You can't scare me!"

"Good lad," said the captain.

"Of course you realize this fellow is missing its stock."

"Its what?" asked Caitlin.

"Its stock," repeated Captain Bowe. "This type of anchor would simply drag without its stock. A length of wood, tapered at both ends, fit into that diamond-shaped hole. The stock forced one of the flukes to dig into the ocean floor." He drew a picture in Caitlin's notebook.

"Did it rot away?" asked Robin.

"Right you are, lad!" said Captain Bowe, patting Robin on the back. "Now for that story I promised."

"First, let's get ourselves ready." He reached into his sea bag and pulled out three yellow oilskins, one for each of the children, and two larger ones for Nicole and himself. Quickly, the children pulled on their raincoats.

"This is weird," whispered Sean.

"Ready," announced Caitlin.

"Something is missing," said Captain Bowe. He reached into the bag and pulled out five sou'westers. Then he dumped the bag upside down. Out tumbled five pairs of rubber boots.

Everyone jumped into their boots.

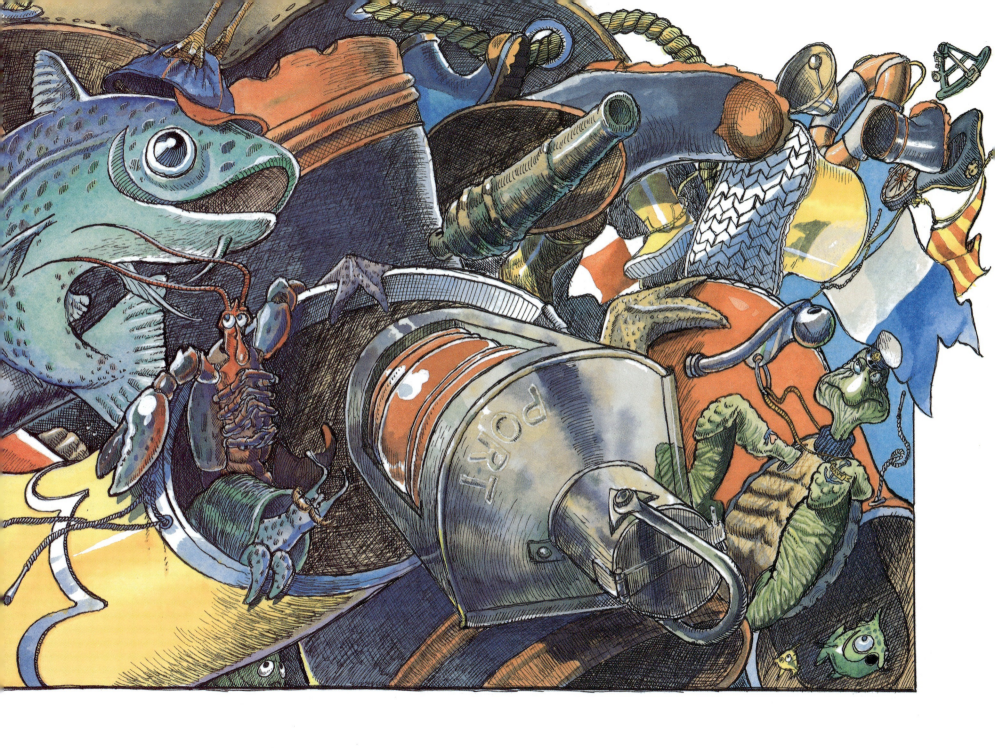

"I remember a story about a lost anchor,"
began the captain. "My grandfather was mate
aboard a fishing schooner out of Lunenburg.

"It was a stormy night, not unusual for that
part of the world, and they were riding at anchor.
Without warning one of those huge ocean liners
loomed out of the darkness, spitting smoke and
cinders into the sky, and acting like she owned
the whole ocean.

"She was heading directly towards them!

"There was no time to raise sail or sound an alarm. My grandfather ran forward, grabbed an axe and cut the anchor cable. The helmsman spun the wheel hard to port, and the vessel fell off to leeward under bare poles. The liner passed so close you could almost have reached out and touched her!"

"They probably never saw that schooner," said Sean.

"Your grandfather was awful lucky," said Robin.

"So true," agreed Captain Bowe. "It gives me the shivers just thinking about it."

"I think your grandfather was very brave and smart," said Caitlin.

"Thank you, little miss," said the captain. "Of course, this anchor may have been lost on a foggy day on the Banks. You know, sometimes the fog out there got so thick you could lean against it. I have heard many a story about fishermen falling right out of their dories because they were caught resting against the fog when it rolled away!"

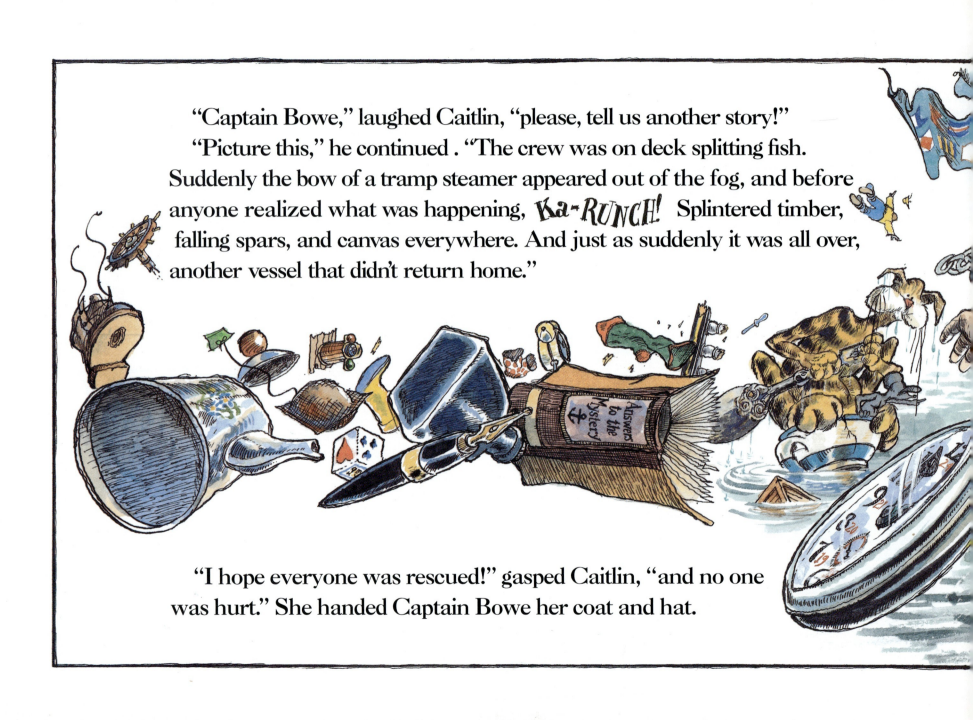

"Captain Bowe," laughed Caitlin, "please, tell us another story!"

"Picture this," he continued . "The crew was on deck splitting fish. Suddenly the bow of a tramp steamer appeared out of the fog, and before anyone realized what was happening, Ka-RUNCH! Splintered timber, falling spars, and canvas everywhere. And just as suddenly it was all over, another vessel that didn't return home."

"I hope everyone was rescued!" gasped Caitlin, "and no one was hurt." She handed Captain Bowe her coat and hat.

Sean looked closely at the anchor with Nicole's magnifying glass. "What is this thing made of?" he asked and then kicked it. Hopping on one foot he cried, "it's hard as rock!!"

"You mean as rigid as wrought iron," said Captain Bowe. "My father used to work in a foundry that forged things out of iron. He was the hammerman! Boy, oh boy, that was another hard and dangerous job." He reached inside his wallet and took out a photograph yellowed with age.

"I remember going with him when I was young and watching him make small anchors. Talk about hot and noisy. That heat could melt your mustache! And I bet one of your rock bands couldn't be heard over the noise made by the huge anchor forge."

"How was the anchor made?" asked Caitlin. She turned to a new page in her notebook. Captain Bowe unwrapped a package of gum. "A bundle of iron bars, like these sticks of gum, was fastened together. Again and again it was swung from furnace to anvil; heated and pounded until the shank was forged. Next, the arms were heated and forged in place."

"Look, I can see where the arms were joined to the shank," said Sean, still looking through the magnifying glass.

"Too much strain on the cable and these arms would break off," said Captain Bowe. "The master of a vessel would not be very happy if he had to buy a new anchor. That would be something he couldn't fix himself."

"Who invented the first anchor?" asked Sean.
"Probably the same person who made the first boat,"
answered Robin with a shrug.
"I wonder what the first anchor looked like?" asked Caitlin.
"Like this, I bet," said Sean. A rock dangled at the end of
his shoelace.

Nicole flipped back the pages of her notebook.
"That's right, Sean. Anchors have been around for
thousands of years. The ancient Egyptians, Greeks,
and Romans used baskets filled with stones and
sacks full of sand."

"How old are these anchors?" asked Robin.

"And how could you three detectives find out?" asked Nicole.

"We could try the Museum!" cried Sean. "I bet there's lots of really neat stuff in there!"

"I'll be there in a minute," said Caitlin. "I just want to check something out." She got a white lab coat from the captain's sea bag.

She marched over to a strange-looking bright red anchor.
She stooped to examine it through her magnifying glass.

She looked...

and she looked...

A Few Words

*Fluke? Sou'wester? You've read some pretty strange words
in this book. Here is what some of them mean.*

Anchor: A heavy object dropped overboard to keep a vessel in one place. Anchors come in different shapes and sizes.  How many anchors can you find in this book? To see the different parts of a fisherman's anchor, look back and find the picture of an anchor in Caitlin's notebook. *Anvil:* A heavy metal block on which metal is shaped by hammering. *Banks:* Shallow areas in the ocean where fish are plentiful. Some famous fishing banks  are the Grand Banks, Georges Bank, and

LaHave Bank. *Bare poles:* When all the sails are taken down,  a ship is said to be "under bare poles." *Bluenose:* Canada's most famous sailing ship, the *Bluenose* was built in Lunenburg, Nova Scotia, in 1921. She was a fishing schooner, but won many races against Canadian and American schooners. Like Robin, you can have a picture of the *Bluenose* for just 10 cents.

Cable: A strong thick rope. The anchor cable that Mr. Bowe's grandfather cut through would have been about 7.5 centimetres thick and 40 metres long. *Canvas:* Strong cotton fabric used for making sails. Sometimes the word canvas is used to mean sails.

Convoy: A group of merchant ships sailing together with naval ships to protect them.

Dory: A small boat with a flat bottom that is used for fishing.

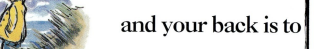

Dories could be stacked like saucers on the decks of a schooner.

Fluke: The part of an anchor arm that digs into the ground. *Leeward:* With your back

to the wind, your front is to leeward 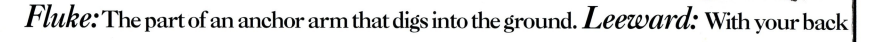 and your back is to

windward. *Master:* The captain of a ship. *Mate:* The second in command on a ship.

Oilskins: In the days before rubber and plastic, waterproof clothing was made by

coating or soaking cloth with linseed oil. Coats, trousers, and sou'westers made of this

material were called oilskins. *Sable Island:* An island made of sand off the coast of

Nova Scotia, famous for its  shipwrecks and wild horses.

Sou'wester: An oilskin hat with a wide slanting brim, longer in the back than the front.

It often has ear flaps that tie under the chin.

Spars: Different poles used to support the rigging on a sailing ship.

Tramp Steamer: A cargo ship that does not make scheduled trips between ports.

Trawler: A fishing boat that catches fish in a big bag-shaped net called a trawl.

THE MARITIME MUSEUM OF THE ATLANTIC

THIS STORY takes place in the Anchor Yard of the Maritime Museum of the Atlantic in downtown Halifax, right on the waterfront.

Inside the museum you can learn lots more about ships and shipwrecks and sailors' lives. You can see figureheads, ship models, and sailboats. Moored alongside the museum is the museum's largest artifact, *CSS Acadia*, a steamship built in 1913.

Dedicated to Alex who taught us that to preserve hope you must
grasp the opportunities to make a difference.—MM